W9-AOI-092

CLOUDY with a chance of MEATBALLS™ TEAMWORK!

by Rebecca Frazer   illustrated by Pete Oswald

Ready-to-Read

Simon Spotlight
New York   London   Toronto   Sydney

SIMON SPOTLIGHT

An imprint of Simon & Schuster
Children's Publishing Division
1230 Avenue of the Americas
New York, New York 10020

TM & © 2009 Sony Pictures Animation, Inc. All rights reserved.

All rights reserved, including the right of reproduction in whole or
in part in any form. SIMON SPOTLIGHT and colophon are registered
trademarks of Simon & Schuster, Inc.

For information about special discounts for bulk purchases, please
contact Simon & Schuster Special Sales at 1-866-506-1949 or
business@simonandschuster.com.

Manufactured in the United States of America

First Edition 10 9 8 7 6 5 4 3 2 1

ISBN 978-1-4169-6735-4

Read the original book by
Judi Barrett and Ron Barrett

Cloudy
With a
Chance of
Meatballs

As far back as he could remember, Flint Lockwood knew he was born to create something awesome.

But most of Flint's inventions
did not work out as he planned.
When this happened, Flint felt
like no one in the world knew
how bad he felt. Not even his dad.

His dad wanted him to stop
inventing things. But Flint never
gave up his dream.
As the years went by,
Flint's ideas got bigger
and his creations became
harder to make.

HAMBURGER

FOOD CODE:
N.//YZBUG/7RU0

Flint now had his heart set on
fixing the town's food problem.
You see, the people of Swallow Falls
only ate sardines! If Flint could
create a delicious food machine,
his dad would be so proud of him!

But there were two problems with this plan. The first was that Flint's inventions always ended in disaster.

The second was that Flint's dad
wanted him to come work with him
at his sardine bait and tackle shop.

TIM'S
AND SON
BAIT

WE HAVE GEAR FOR
EVERY
SARDINE FISHING
NEED

So Flint went to work at the shop.
But little did anyone know, he was
getting ready to reveal a secret
new invention—a machine that could
make any kind of food on the spot!

Flint knew he could get his machine
to work if he had more power. So he
connected it to the town's power
station. But that was too powerful.
The machine blasted into the clouds!

Thanks to the machine, it started raining food—no more sardines! The weather forecast was always delicious. It rained pizza, it poured pepperoni, and it drizzled jelly beans!

Everyone loved the new weather.
Everyone except Flint's dad.

When it came to Flint's inventions, they never saw eye to eye. But this time it did not bother Flint. He had other things on his mind—like the new friends he was making.

Flint was also enjoying being a star around town. Even the mayor wanted to be his friend. No one made fun of Flint's failed inventions anymore.

While Flint was busy being famous,
his dad went on worrying.

He did not want Flint's
invention to end in disaster.
In fact, he wanted Flint to
turn off the machine!

But Flint was happy that the townspeople liked him now.

He told his dad that his fate was
not to be tacked to a tackle shop,
but to be an inventor.
Then he headed back
to his lab in a huff.

Back in his lab, Flint's sour mood
turned sweet when the mayor
called him the town hero.
The machine would not be shut down—
even though the food was gigantic!

DANGEOMETER

But the food kept getting bigger.
It turned out that Flint's machine
was out of control. It had created
the perfect food storm everywhere.
The world was in danger!

Flint felt flattened by
the machine's giant food.
He finally thought his dad
might be right—he was a failure.
Just then Flint's dad came to talk
with him. He did not think Flint
was a failure, he believed in him!

So Flint put on his lab coat
and went to work.
But the town was now against him
and he only had one fan—his dad.

Flint was off to shut down the
machine and save the world.
Nothing could get in his way—
except that he forgot the
Shutdown Recipe! His dad would
have to figure out how to
e-mail it to Flint!

Flint's dad did not want
to let him down, so he followed
Flint's e-mail instructions.
When he was just about
to hit SEND, an enormous
banana knocked him out.

To Flint's surprise, his dad managed to send a special delivery—the e-mail he needed!

With the Shutdown Recipe,
Flint rushed full-speed through
a tunnel toward the machine.
It was time to save the world!

Too bad Flint's dad
e-mailed him the wrong file!
Without the Shutdown Recipe,
Flint and the world were doomed.

But Flint had his mind
set on saving the world.
He knew he needed to come up
with a way—and he did!
He used Spray-On Shoes,
one of his old inventions,
to seal the spout of his machine!

Bursting with pride and love,
Flint's dad was ready to celebrate
with the town hero . . . his son.
"I'm proud of you, son," he said.
"I love you."
"I love you too, Dad!" Flint said.